15.00

FEATHER
TALES

Storky Stork

David M. Sargent, Jr., and his friends live in Northwest Arkansas. His writing career began in 1995 with a cruel joke being played on his mother. The friends pictured with him are (from left to right), Vera, Buffy, and Mary.

Dave Sargent is a lifelong resident of the small town of Prairie Grove, Arkansas. A fourth-generation dairy farmer, Dave began writing in early December, 1990. He enjoys the outdoors and has a real love for birds and animals.

Storky Stork

By

Dave Sargent

Illustrated by
Jane Lenoir

Ozark Publishing, Inc.
P.O. Box 228
Prairie Grove, AR 72753

Library of Congress cataloging-in-publication data

Sargent, Dave, 1941—
    Storky Stork / by Dave Sargent ; illustrated by Jane
Lenoir.
    p. cm
    Summary: Storky Stork helps ornery Billy Goat when
his bad actions and attitude cause everyone to lose trust
in him. Includes factual information about storks.
    ISBN 1-56763-467-2 -- ISBN 1-56763-468-0 9pbk.)
    [1. Trust--Fiction. 2. Behavior--Fiction. 3. Goats--
Fiction 4. Storks--Fiction.] I. Lenoir, Jane, 1950- ill. II.
Title.

PZ7S.2465 St 2000
[Fic]--dc21
                                                00-0200697

Printed in the United States of America

iv

Inspired by

an occasional glimpse of a beautiful stork. They are very proud birds.

Dedicated to

all students, big and small, who have been told that the stork brings babies. Some think this is an old wives' tale. But it's not. This is a true legend which arises from the fact that storks take very loving care of their own young.

Foreword

Storky teaches Billy Goat the true meaning of trust. When someone trusts you, don't destroy that trust—unless that animal or person is doing something that would hurt others. Then, it's okay to tell. Maintaining someone's trust is easy. Regaining someone's trust is hard.

Contents

Storky Stork

If you would like to have an author of The Feather Tale Series visit your school, free of charge, just call 1-800-321-5671 or 1-800-960-3876.

One

King of the Barnyard?

Sunlight danced upon the wet marshlands of Louisiana and slowly warmed the cooler temperatures of the night. Storky Stork stood amid the tall reeds and gazed at the calm surface of the water. He yawned and stretched his large black tapering flight wings. And, after preening the white feathers on his back and under-belly, he felt he was ready to meet the day with confidence.

"I'd really like to meet some new friends today," Storky muttered.

"Mine are all busy with their normal routine. I think it's time for me to take a little vacation." He chuckled as he added, "If only for a few hours, I would really enjoy seeing new and different lands! That's what I'll do. I'll fly away to someplace new."

And a moment later, Storky was airborne. His alert eyes scanned the ground below as he flew northward. His blackish, bare-skinned head and neck with his long, narrow bill held at a proud angle were really a picturesque sight.

Storky's flight was taking him over tall trees and manicured, very well-kept farmland when a loud noise suddenly seized his attention. First, he made a wide circle, then came in low and swooped even lower for a closer look.

"So! I don't care if Farmer John trusts me or not," the voice bellowed. "It's more fun to have everybody wonder what you're gonna do next!"

"Hmmm," Storky murmured. "What a strange attitude!"

The large, long-legged bird landed on a tree stump near the little audience. He watched quietly for a moment as the cynical talker pawed the ground with one little hoof and shook his head in defiance.

"I am Billy Goat, King of the Barnyard," he said.

"But, we just don't trust you, Billy," a small voice replied.

"We never know how you're going to treat us," another said. "Sometimes you are very nice, and sometimes you hurt us with bad words or you butt us with your head.

4

You're not King of the Barnyard.
You're not even our trusted friend!"

Billy Goat downed his head and ran back and forth through the group of onlookers. They scurried away.

"Shame on you, Billy Goat," Storky boomed, "for being so ornery and untrustworthy."

"Hey! Who said that?" the goat yelled, as he whirled around several times, looking for the new voice.

"I did," the stork said, "and I'll say it again. Shame on you!"

"I will," Billy Goat growled, "do and say exactly what I want, and not you or anyone else can stop me."

Only seconds later, the ornery little goat was thundering toward Storky Stork with his head down. And everyone could tell that Billy meant business.

"You certainly are determined to be a bad little critter," Storky Stork chuckled as he flapped his large black wings and slowly sailed above the head of the angry goat.

"Your attitude is terrible," the
bird said as he landed a safe distance
from Billy.

Two

Billy Butts Farmer John

"Bah!" the little goat bawled. "Bah to trust! Bah to being nice! And bah to friends! I am Billy Goat! I don't need anybody!"

The enraged goat turned and ran toward the barnyard. Farmer John was bent over, quietly feeding the chickens.

"Now, there's a good target," the ill-tempered little goat growled. "If they don't think I'm important, I'll show them! I'll show everybody that I am king of this barnyard!"

Storky gulped and closed his eyes as Billy hit the man with a thud. Farmer John sailed, head first, through the fence of the chicken pen.

The posts snapped off at the ground, and the chicken wire landed in a tangled heap on top of him. Chickens squawked and flew over Farmer John's prone body.

As feathers and dust settled, the animals grouped around the dazed man and groaned.

"Farmer John is good to us," a voice cried. "Why did you butt him, Billy? He feeds and cares for us."

"Uh oh," Storky Stork gasped. "This time Billy Goat has gone too far with his bad attitude and his untrustworthy habits. I just hope he didn't hurt Farmer John!"

Suddenly the door of the farmhouse flew open, and Molly stood on the steps, straining her eyes to see what was happening. Her gaze stopped on the man who was now covered with the debris from the wrecked chicken pen.

"John!" Molly screamed as she ran toward him. "Are you all right?"

Tears streamed down her face as she knelt beside Farmer John. He was dusted, feathered, and bruised. He groaned and tried to sit up.

"Don't try to move, John," Molly cried. "I'll telephone for help. You may have broken some bones."

Farmer John gasped for air before finally getting enough to speak. "You mean Billy may have broken some of my bones. I knew I should never trust that bad-attitude little goat!" he whispered hoarsely.

"Billy did this to you?" Molly asked.

Farmer John murmured, "Yeah, he did. Don't telephone for help yet, Molly. I think I'll be able to get up in a minute."

Molly glanced around and saw the goat peering at them from behind the chicken house.

"You get away from us!" Molly yelled at Billy. "John trusted you, and now look! You hurt him! Shoo, you bad-tempered critter! Shoo!"

Billy Goat turned away from the scene and walked across the clearing toward the woods with his little head down. He no longer looked arrogant and ready for battle. Farmer John and Molly would hate him now. Storky saw a tear slowly trickle down Billy's face and fall to the ground.

The stork watched Billy until the goat reached the edge of the woods. Billy paused and looked back at the damage he had done before disappearing amid the trees.

He needs time, Storky thought, to think about the consequences of his disloyalty and rudeness.

Now, perhaps he'll understand the pain that he causes with his bad actions and attitude. Perhaps he's ready to change the bad to good!

Seconds later, the big stork was airborne, flying at high speed toward the little goat.

"Hey, Billy!" he yelled. "Wait! I need to talk to you!"

The big bird glided downward, landing mere inches from the goat.

"Aren't you afraid that I'll hurt you?" the little critter whimpered.

"No," Storky replied in a firm voice. "I'm not afraid that you'll hurt me. I think you are feeling sorry about your last tantrum."

The little billy goat sniffled and hiccuped. He rubbed his eyes against his front leg before looking at Storky.

"I'm sorry I didn't listen to you earlier," he murmured. "No one will ever trust me again now."

All of a sudden big tears poured down Billy's face. He cried so hard that his little shoulders trembled like a leaf in the wind.

"Storky," he mumbled, "I want to be trusted. I want to have friends. I want to be a good little goat."

The big bird sighed and smiled. He nodded his head and patted Billy on the shoulder with his wing.

"I know you do, Billy" he said. "And I think I have a plan that will let everyone know your new feelings. Listen closely. I want you to . . ."

Three

Farmer John's Cast

Storky watched as Molly helped Farmer John into the truck. A few moments later, the vehicle rumbled down the lane to the main road and sped toward town.

"Okay, Billy," he said with a smile. "It's time to go to work."

The little billy goat smiled and nodded his head.

"I'm ready, Storky," Billy said. "And I intend to prove to everyone that I have turned over a new leaf." He giggled, "I mean I've turned on a

new attitude. I'm going to be trust-
worthy and kind to everybody!"

"Is that all?" Storky asked in a
stern voice.

"No, Mr. Storky," Billy replied.
"I'm going to work real hard to repair
the damage I did to the chicken pen."

"And?" Storky asked.

"And I'm going to prove to
Farmer John that I can be trusted,"
Billy said. "Boy, that's going to be
the hardest part of this whole thing."

"You're right," Storky said.
"Regaining trust is a lot harder than
maintaining it. Now, go to work."

Billy scampered to the chicken
pen and started to pull the broken
fence away from the outbuildings.
All of a sudden, he noticed that ole
Barney the Bear Killer was helping
him. The goat offered a smile of

gratitude, and Barney grinned before sinking his teeth into another post. They carefully began to straighten each bent wire into its original shape.

Meanwhile, Storky Stork had gathered the animals into a group. He explained the change in Billy's attitude and politely asked for their assistance in repairing the damages.

Storky lined up the menagerie. He asked each one about their special talent before assigning a duty.

Within a short time, Marty Mule was moving the rest of the broken poles into a pile. Billy Beaver was cutting the jagged ends off each pole and smoothing out the rough edges. Tom Gopher and his brothers were digging up the broken ends and cleaning the dirt and damaged wood from the post holes. The chickens cleaned up the scattered feathers and dust from the pen. They all worked hard, and, some three hours later, Marty Mule hoisted the last pole into an upright position between two pigs, and Billy Goat butted the bottom of it until it fell down into the hole. The little gophers were busy packing dirt around each upright post.

Billy, Barney, and Marty Mule replaced the chicken wire into its proper position on the poles, and the duck and goose carefully looped pieces of wire around in various spots to hold it in place.

When the chicken pen was all finished, Billy thanked everyone and apologized to every member of the barnyard family.

"I'll never abuse your trust again," Billy Goat said. "My heart feels happier when I'm nice and kind and honest. I am one happy-hearted goat right now! Thanks for helping me put my life back on track."

All the animals congratulated Billy and cheered in agreement. And Barney the Bear Killer howled a big "You're welcome!"

Suddenly the sound of a vehicle interrupted the little celebration.

"Oh, dear," Billy Goat groaned. "Farmer John is back. I sure hope he forgives me."

Storky rested his wing on the goat. "Just apologize and don't ever act that way again," he murmured.

"Okay, everyone," Storky Stork yelled. "Get out of sight. Hurry!"

The truck stopped in front of the house, and Farmer John and Molly got out of it. He had a white cast on his arm and a sling around his neck.

Suddenly, they stared toward the chicken pen. Their eyes widened at the wonder before them. The pen was in perfect condition, and young Billy Goat was kneeling with his face resting on the ground.

"Oh, look at Billy," Molly said. "He's trying to tell you he's sorry."

Billy goat nodded his head and bleated softly.

As they slowly walked toward him, Farmer John murmured, "Okay, I accept your apology, Billy. I'll put my trust in you again. What I can't figure is how you repaired all the damage by yourself. You've never had that many friends."

Billy nestled his head against the man's pants leg.

Storky breathed a sigh of relief before quickly taking flight toward Louisiana. As he flew southward, his mind drifted back over the events of the day.

"Well," he murmured. "I wanted to meet new friends, and I certainly did that. I think Billy Goat can be trusted now. But he won't forget again, will he?" Hmmm . . .

Four

Stork Facts

Stork is the name of a group of birds with long legs, strong wings, and a long, pointed beak.

There are 17 species of storks throughout the world--14 in the eastern hemisphere and three in the western hemisphere. Storks feed on insects, fish, frogs, reptiles, young birds, and small mammals. Most species of storks look for food in swamps and marshes, but some species hunt in grassy plains and farm fields.

Jabiru

Saddle-billed
Stork

Lesser
Adjutant

Black
Stork

The best-known stork, the white stork, lives in parts of Europe, Asia and northern Africa in the summer and in Africa, northern India and southern China in the winter. This stork is white with black markings on its wings. It has a red beak, and its legs and feet are a reddish-pink.

White storks frequently nest on roofs and chimneys. A pair of storks will return to the same nest year after year. The white stork is a respected and protected bird in many places. It is a common belief that this beautiful white stork brings good luck. The legend that we are familiar with, that the stork brings the new baby into the home, arises from the fact that the bird takes loving care of its young.

Other storks of the eastern hemisphere include the marabou, the black stork, and the woolly-necked stork. The maguari stork and the jabiru, a bird that measures five feet in height, live in Central and South America.

The wood stork, formerly called the wood ibis, is the only true stork native to the United States. It lives in the cypress swamps of Florida, as well as coastal regions of Central and South America. This large, white bird stands about 3 1/2 feet tall. The undersides of the wings are mostly black, as are the tail feathers. The number of wood storks in Florida declined dramatically during the mid-1900's, mainly because of the loss of swamp lands where the birds fed.

Scientific Classification:
Storks make up the stork family, *Ciconiidae*. The white stork is *Ciconia ciconia*, the wood stork Mycteria americana.

J
Sargent